ROADRUNNER'S DANCE

by Rudolfo Anaya

Pictures by
David Diaz

Hyperion Books for Children
New York

For information address Hyperion Books for Children, 114 Fifth Avenue, New York, New York 10011-5690.
Printed in Singapore
First Edition
3 5 7 9 10 8 6 4
This book is set in 17-point Goudy

Library of Congress Cataloging-in-Publication Data
Anaya, Rudolfo A.
Roadrunner's dance / by Rudolfo Anaya ; pictures by David Diaz.
p. cm.
Summary: Because Rattlesnake has taken over the road and will not let any of the people or animals in the village use it, Desert Woman enlists the aid of the other animals to create a strange new creature with the necessary tools to overcome Rattlesnake.
ISBN 0-7868-0254-5 (trade) / ISBN 0-7868-2209-0 (lib.)
[1. Roadrunner—Fiction. 2. Rattlesnakes—Fiction. 3. Desert animals—Fiction. 4. Southwest, New—Fiction.] I. Diaz, David, ill. II. Title.
PZ7.A5186 Ro 2000
[Fic]—dc21
99-89871

Visit www.hyperionchildrensbooks.com

To the animals of our desert Southwest

—R.A.

For Erika

—D.D.

"Ssss," hissed Snake as he slithered out of his hole by the side of the road. He bared his fangs and frightened a family walking home from the cornfield.

The mother threw her basketful of corn in the air. The children froze with fright.

"Father!" the children called, and the father came running.

"Sssss," Snake threatened.

"Come away," the father said, and the family took another path home.

"I am king of the road," Snake boasted. "No one may use the road without my permission."

That evening the people of the village gathered together and spoke to the elders.

"We are afraid of being bitten by Snake," they protested. "He acts as if the road belongs only to him."

The elders agreed that something should be done, and so the following morning they went to Sacred Mountain, where Desert Woman lived. She had created the desert animals, so surely she could help.

"Please do something about Snake," the elders said. "He makes visiting our neighbors and going to our fields impossible. He frightens the children."

Desert Woman thought for a long time. She did not like to interfere in the lives of the people and animals, but she knew that something must be done.

"I have a solution," she finally said.

Dressed in a flowing gown, she traveled on a summer cloud across the desert to where Snake slept under the shade of a rocky ledge.

"You will let people know when you are about to strike," Desert Woman said sternly. And so she placed a rattle on the tip of Snake's tail.

"Now you are Rattlesnake. When anyone approaches, you will rattle a warning. This way they will know you are nearby."

Convinced she had done the right thing, Desert Woman walked on the Rainbow back to her home in Sacred Mountain.

However, instead of inhibiting Rattlesnake, the rattle only made him more threatening. He coiled around, shaking his tail and baring his fangs.

"Look at me," Rattlesnake said to the animals. "I rattle and hiss, and my bite is deadly. I am king of the road, and no one may use it without my permission!"

Now the animals went to Desert Woman to complain.

"*Who, who,*" Owl said, greeting Desert Woman with respect. "Since you gave Rattlesnake his rattle, he is even more of a bully. He will not let anyone use the road. Please take away his fangs and rattle!"

"What I give I cannot take away," Desert Woman said. "When Rattlesnake comes hissing and threatening, one of you must make him behave."

She looked at all the animals assembled. The animals looked at one another. They looked up, they looked down, but not one looked at Desert Woman.

"I am too timid to stand up to Rattlesnake," Quail whispered.

"He would gobble me up," Lizard cried and darted away.

"We are all afraid of him," Owl admitted.

Desert Woman smiled. "Perhaps we need a new animal to make Rattlesnake behave," she suggested.

"Yip, yip," Coyote barked. "Yes, yes."

"If you help me, together we can make a guardian of the road," Desert Woman said. "I will form the body, and each of you will bring a gift for our new friend."

She gathered clay from the Sacred Mountain and wet it with water from a desert spring. Working quickly but with great care, she molded the body.

"He needs slender legs to run fast," said Deer. He took two slender branches from a mesquite bush and handed them to Desert Woman.

She pushed the sticks into the clay.

"And a long tail to balance himself," said Blue Jay.

"Caw, Caw! Like mine," croaked Raven, and he took long, black feathers from his tail.

"He must be strong," cried the mighty Eagle, and he plucked dark feathers from his wings.

"And have a long beak to peck at Rattlesnake," said Heron, offering a long, thin reed from the marsh.

"He needs sharp eyes," said Coyote, offering two shiny stones from the riverbed.

As Desert Woman added each new gift to the clay body, a strange new bird took shape.

"What is your gift?" Owl asked Desert Woman.

"I will give him the gift of dance. He will be agile and fast," she answered. "I will call him Roadrunner."

Then she breathed life into the clay.

Roadrunner opened his eyes. He blinked and looked around.

"What a strange bird," the animals said.

Roadrunner took his first steps. He tottered forward, then backward, then forward, and fell flat on his face.

The animals sighed and shook their heads. This bird was not agile, and he was not fast. He could never stand up to Rattlesnake. He was too awkward. Disappointed, the animals made their way home.

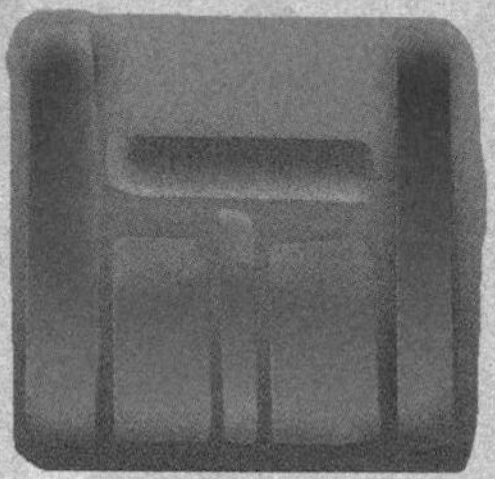

Desert Woman helped Roadrunner stand, and she told him what he must do. "You will dance around Rattlesnake and peck at his tail. He must learn he is not the king of the road."

"Me? Can I really do it?" Roadrunner asked, balancing himself with his long tail.

"You need only to practice," Desert Woman said.

Roadrunner again tried his legs. He took a few steps forward and bumped into a tall cactus.

"Practice," he said. He tried again and leaped over a sleeping horned toad.

He tried jumping over a desert tortoise, but landed right on her back. The surprised turtle lumbered away, and Roadrunner crashed to the ground.

"I'll never get it right," he moaned.

"Yes, you will," Desert Woman said, again helping him to his feet. "You need only to practice."

So Roadrunner practiced. He ran back and forth, learning to use his skinny legs, learning to balance with his tail feathers.

"Practice," he said again. "Practice."

With time, he was swirling and twirling like a twister. The once awkward bird was now a graceful dancer.

"I've got it!" he cried, zipping down the road, his legs carrying him swiftly across the sand. "Thank you, Desert Woman."

"Use your gift to help others," Desert Woman said, and she returned to her abode on Sacred Mountain.

"I will," Roadrunner called.

He went racing down the road until his sharp eyes spied Rattlesnake hiding under a tall yucca plant.

"*Sssss*, I am king of the road," Rattlesnake hissed and shook his tail furiously. "No one may use *my* road without *my* permission."

"The road is for everyone to use," Roadrunner said sternly.

"Who are you?"

"I am Roadrunner."

"Get off my road before I bite you!" Rattlesnake glared.

"I'm not afraid of you," Roadrunner replied.

The people and the animals heard the ruckus and drew close to watch. Had they heard correctly? Roadrunner was challenging Rattlesnake!

"I'll show you I *am* king of the road!" Rattlesnake shouted, hissing so loud the desert mice trembled with fear. He shook his rattle until it sounded like a thunderstorm.

He struck at Roadrunner, but Roadrunner hopped out of the way.

"Stand still!" Rattlesnake cried and lunged again.

But Roadrunner danced gracefully out of reach.

Rattlesnake coiled for one more attempt. He struck like lightning, but fell flat on his face. Roadrunner had jumped to safety.

Now it was Roadrunner's turn. He ruffled his feathers and danced in circles around Rattlesnake. Again and again he pecked at the bully's tail. Like a whirlwind, he spun around Rattlesnake until the serpent grew dizzy. His eyes grew crossed and his tongue hung limply out of his mouth.

"You win! You win!" Rattlesnake cried.

"You are not king of the road, and you must not frighten those who use it," Roadrunner said sternly.

"I promise, I promise," the beaten Rattlesnake said and quietly slunk down his hole.

The people cheered and praised the bird.

"Now we can visit out neighbors in peace and go to our cornfields without fear!" the elders proclaimed. "And the children will no longer be frightened."

"Thank you, Roadrunner!" the children called, waving as they followed their parents to the fields.

Then the animals gathered around Roadrunner.

"Yes, thank you for teaching Rattlesnake a lesson," Owl said. "Now you are king of the road."

"No, now there is no king of the road," replied Roadrunner. "Everyone is free to come and go as they please. And the likes of Rattlesnake had better watch out, because I'll make sure the roads stay safe."

AUTHOR'S NOTE

To this day roadrunners help keep roads and paths clear of rattlesnakes. However, they too have to be careful, because today some of the old roads of the people of New Mexico are superhighways. Cars and trucks race along them. Roadrunners have learned to look both ways before they cross.

Roadrunners love to be around people. Last year two roadrunners built their nest in a Russian olive tree in our backyard. Both parents took care of the nest, and when the eggs hatched, they cared tenderly for their young. When the birds left the nest, the parents taught the little ones to look both ways before crossing the street.

This story emerged from my interest in creation stories. Creation stories tell us how things began. What if the first roadrunner was created by a committee of animals? I thought. In the committee, each animal would contribute his own idea of what would make the new bird unique. The outcome could be really weird. Fortunately, Desert Woman helps, and gives Roadrunner the gift of dance.

Some people think roadrunners are awkward birds because of their appearance, but they are nimble creatures that have a role in nature. Every living creature has a special gift. We all need to find our abilities and use them wisely. And, like Roadrunner, we need to keep practicing our talents so we don't get rusty.

R.A.